Timothy Todd's Good Things Are Gone

ANNE ROCKWELL

MACMILLAN PUBLISHING CO., INC.
New York

Macmillan Publishing Co., Inc.
866 Third Avenue, New York, N.Y. 10022
Collier Macmillan Canada, Ltd.

Printed in the United States of America

10   9   8   7   6   5   4   3   2   1

LIBRARY OF CONGRESS CATALOGING IN PUBLICATION DATA
Rockwell, Anne F.
   Timothy Todd's good things are gone.
   (Ready-to-read)
   SUMMARY: A country peddler looks for clues which will
lead him to his missing pack.
   [1. Peddlers and peddling—Fiction] I. Title.
PZ7.R5943Ti   [E]   78-6299   ISBN 0-02-777600-X

For Hannah,

Elizabeth

and Oliver

CHAPTER ONE

Timothy Todd was
a peddler.
Timothy Todd's pack
was full of good things
to sell.

5

There were books and balls,

molasses, needles and nails.

There were satin ribbons

and calico cloth.

There were pots and pans

and scissors and thread.

There was sweet candy

and a shiny new harmonica

and many more good things.

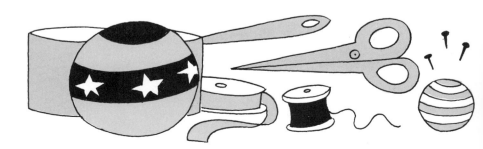

"Oh, what good things
   I have this week,"
   said Timothy Todd.
"I will sell these things
   to Miller Moore
   and Widow Wilson
   and Farmer Foote.
   I will sell them
   to Lizzy and Lucy and Jack.
   I will sell
   so many good things
   that I will get rich."

Timothy Todd felt
a drop of rain.
He felt another.
Soon it was raining hard.

"Oh, shucks,"
  said Timothy Todd.
"Now it is raining
  and all my good things
  will get wet.
  I will get wet, too."
  Timothy Todd ran off the road.
  He ran into the deep woods.
  Just then he heard thunder.
  Just then he saw lightning.
"Oh, my!" said Timothy Todd.
"I am scared!"
  He ran deeper into the woods.

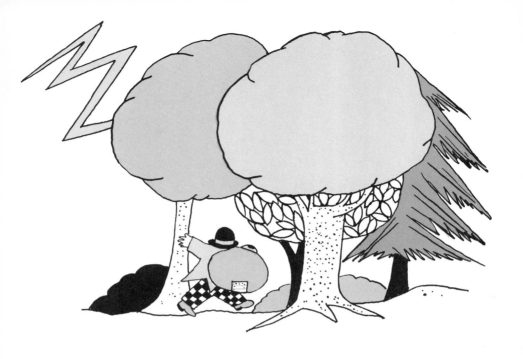

CHAPTER TWO

Timothy Todd ran.

It rained.

It thundered.

More lightning lit the sky.

Suddenly Timothy Todd
saw something.
It was old.
It was ugly.
It was a little house.
"That little house looks
old and ugly,
but it looks like a good place
to go in the rain,"
said Timothy Todd.
So Timothy Todd ran to
the little house.

The door was open

but there was no one inside.

Timothy Todd looked around.

There were cobwebs in the corners.

There was a fireplace

and some dry wood.

There was a pot and a pan

and a dish and a spoon.

13

There was no one in the little house,
and it was raining outside.
"Perhaps someone lived in
this little house long ago,"
said Timothy Todd.
"Now there is no one here but me.
I will build a fire
and dry my feet.
I will eat some candy
and read a good book.
Then I will go to sleep.
Morning will come soon.
And I will not be scared."

More thunder came.

More lightning did, too.

It rained harder and harder.

Timothy Todd dried his feet,

ate some candy

and read a good book

about a detective named Sam.

He put his pack full of good things
next to him
and went to sleep.
It rained and rained.

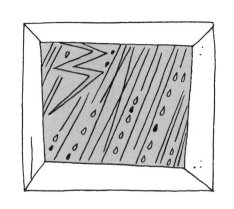

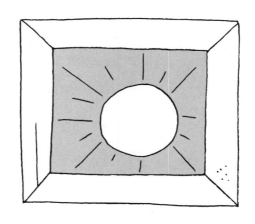

CHAPTER THREE

Morning came.

So did the sun.

It was not raining.

Timothy Todd woke up.

He saw his hat.

He saw his shoes.

But he did not see his pack.

He looked in every corner
of the little old house.
He saw cobwebs in every corner,
but he did not see his pack.
He looked up and down
and all around,
but he did not see his pack.

"My pack cannot walk,"
  said Timothy Todd.
"It cannot fly.
  It cannot go away by itself.
  So someone must have taken it.
  But who?
  That is a mystery.
  I wish I were a detective
  like Sam in that good book
  I read last night.
  Sam looked for clues.
  He found them.
  I wish I could, too."

Timothy Todd looked sad.

He thought and thought.

"But I can pretend,"
said Timothy Todd.

"I will pretend
I am a detective like Sam.

I will look for clues.

I will try to find my pack."

Timothy Todd looked.

Suddenly he saw a clue.

He saw some fur.

It was bear fur.

"Oh, my," said Timothy Todd.

"Perhaps the bear took my pack.

I am scared of bears.

But I must find my pack!"

Timothy Todd walked
deeper into the woods.
"Bears live in caves,"
said Timothy Todd.
"So if I find a cave,
perhaps I will find the bear.
Perhaps I will find my pack."

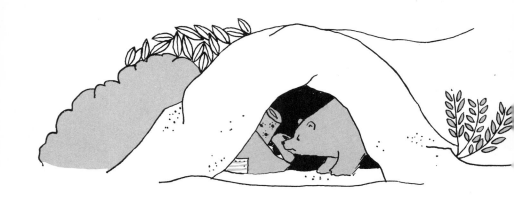

CHAPTER FOUR

"But what if I find a cave,
and in that cave
I find the bear
with my pack?
What if I ask for my pack
and the bear will not
give it back?

What if it growls
and shakes its head?
What then?
Poor me!"
Timothy Todd got very scared.

Just then he heard
something growl.
Timothy Todd hid
behind a tree.
He saw something.
It was growling.
But it was not a bear.

It was a bobcat.

It was not growling

at Timothy Todd.

It was growling

at a big ball.

It was growling as it played

with the big ball.

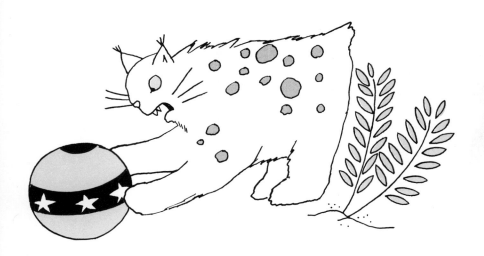

"That big ball was
in my pack,"
said Timothy Todd.
"So it was not the bear
who took my pack.
It was the bobcat.
While the bobcat is playing
with the ball,
I will sneak away.
I will sneak away
very quietly, and I will find
the bobcat's tracks.
The ground is muddy,
so there will be tracks.

I will follow those tracks
until I find my pack.
Oh, what a good detective I am!"

The bobcat growled loudly
as it played with the big ball.
The bobcat growled so loudly,
it did not hear Timothy Todd
sneak away.

CHAPTER FIVE

Timothy Todd found the tracks.

He followed them.

He followed them to a tree.

Then there were

no more tracks.

"I think the bobcat
   went up this tree,"
   said Timothy Todd.
"Perhaps my pack
   is up in the tree."
   Timothy Todd climbed the tree.

His pack was not there.
Just then a crow
flew out of the tree.
"Caw! Caw!" it said.
It had a satin ribbon,
a satin ribbon
from Timothy Todd's pack.

Timothy Todd looked down
from the tree.
He could see the little old house.
He had come back
where he started,
but he had not found his pack.
Then Timothy Todd
saw the bear.

The bear was sitting by
the little old house.
The bear was drinking something.
"Slurp, slurp,"
said the bear
as it drank the good, sweet molasses
from Timothy Todd's pack.

"When the bear goes away,"
said Timothy Todd,
"I must follow it.
I think it will lead me
to my pack."

"Umph," said the bear
as it licked its paws.
It drank up all the molasses
and walked away.
But Timothy Todd
did not follow the bear.

He did not follow the bear
because he heard something.
Someone was playing a tune
on a harmonica.
The tune was coming from
inside the little old house.
Timothy Todd climbed down
from the tree.
He sneaked up to the window
of the little old house.

CHAPTER SIX

Timothy Todd saw his pack.
It was empty.
Good things were
all over the floor.

An old man sat
in the little house.
He was playing a tune
on a shiny new harmonica.

The old man stopped playing.
He looked at Timothy Todd.
"Who are you?" he asked.
"I am Timothy Todd, the peddler,"
  said Timothy Todd.
"That is my pack,
  and all those good things
  are mine."
"That is true,"
  said the old man.
"And this is my little house.
  It is not a hotel.

You spent the night in
my little house,
so I took your pack.
Fair is fair.

42

I do not like peddlers.

I do not like people.

I like the bear

and the bobcat and the crow.

They do not bother me,

and I do not bother them.

I like the deep woods,

and I like my own little house.

Late last night I came home

to my own little house.

A peddler was sleeping there.

I did not like that.

And that peddler was snoring.

While the peddler slept and snored,

I took the pack full of good things.

I gave some good things
to the bear, the bobcat
and the crow.
I kept the harmonica for myself
because I liked the harmonica best.
I have not played a pretty tune
in many years."
He began to play the tune again.

CHAPTER SEVEN

"Listen," said Timothy Todd,
"I have a good idea.
Your house is not a hotel.
That is true.
But we can pretend something."
The old man said,
"I have not pretended
for a very long time.
Perhaps I have forgotten how."

"Oh, no," said Timothy Todd.
"You never forget how to pretend.
I pretended I was a detective,
and I found my pack.
Now we can pretend
your little house
is a hotel.
Then I can pay you
for sleeping here."
"What will you pay me?"
asked the old man.

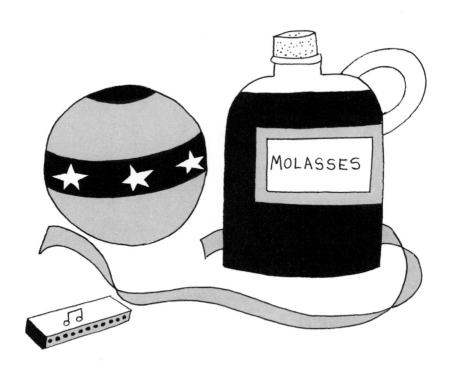

"I will pay you with one big ball,
one satin ribbon,
some good, sweet molasses
and one shiny new harmonica,"
said Timothy Todd.

"No, that is not enough,"
the old man said.
Timothy Todd thought.

"Well," he said,
"then I will pay you
   with some candy,
   good, sweet candy.
   Let me see.
   I have chocolate bars,
   lollipops or lemon drops.
   Take your choice."
"I do not like candy,"
   the old man said.
"But I would like
   a good book to read
   when it rains or snows."

Timothy Todd gave him
the book about
the detective named Sam.
Then Timothy Todd began
to pick up his things.
The old man
did not say anything.

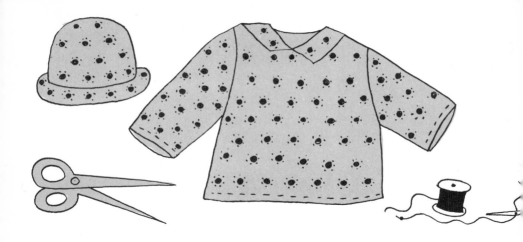

Timothy Todd picked up
the calico cloth.
"That is pretty calico cloth,"
said the old man.
"If I had some scissors
and a needle and thread,
I could make a new shirt
for me.
Perhaps I could make
a new hat, too."

"Yes," said Timothy Todd.
"That is true.
But I promised this calico cloth
to Widow Wilson.
I do not have any for you."
"Shucks!" said the old man.

"But listen,"
said Timothy Todd.
"I have another good idea.
I will pass through
these deep woods again.
Perhaps it will rain.
Perhaps it will snow.
Perhaps the bear
and the bobcat
will bother me.

If you would let me
spend the night
in your little house
and sit by your nice, warm fire,
I would bring you
some calico cloth."

"That is a good idea,"
the old man said.
"We could pretend
my little house is a hotel.
A little hotel."

Timothy Todd picked up his pack.
He said,
"If you will give me
   some supper and breakfast
   when I come again,
   I will give you some scissors
   and a needle and thread."

"Oh, yes," said the old man,
"I will do that."
And he picked up
the harmonica
and began to play
another pretty tune.
Timothy Todd went
out the door.
"Good-by," he said.
"I will come again."

"I like blue,"
    said the old man.
"I like blue calico cloth
    best of all.
    Don't forget."

"I won't forget,"
said Timothy Todd.
"Blue calico cloth."

And away went Timothy Todd,
carrying his pack
full of good things to sell.

ANNE ROCKWELL'S imaginative stories and pictures for young children have made her one of the most popular author/illustrators today. Her Ready-to-Read books for beginning readers include *The Gollywhopper Egg*; *A Bear, A Bobcat and Three Ghosts* (both about the peddler Timothy Todd); *Big Boss* and *The Story Snail*.

With her artist husband Harlow Rockwell, she has created three early-concept picture books, *The Toolbox*, *Thruway* and *Machines*.

Anne Rockwell, her husband and their three children live in Connecticut.

Ready for fun?

Laugh with  **Ready-to-Read** *rib-ticklers.*

5 MEN UNDER 1 UMBRELLA
And Other Ready-to-Read Riddles
Written and illustrated by Joseph Low

Thirty ridiculous riddles will keep beginning readers on their toes. "An enjoyable addition to the abundant volumes of riddle lore." —*Horn Book*

HOMER THE HUNTER
By Richard J. Margolis/Illustrated by Leonard Kessler

The animals Homer the hunter thinks he has killed come back to "haunt" him. "Kids will love 'Ooooooooooing' with the ghosts and find the text easy and satisfying." —*School Library Journal*

GRANNY AND THE INDIANS
By Peggy Parish/Illustrated by Brinton Turkle

Spunky Granny Guntry drives her neighbors, the Indians, frantic in "an original, truly funny story...." —*Horn Book*

GRANNY AND THE DESPERADOES
By Peggy Parish/Illustrated by Steven Kellogg

Granny Guntry confronts two pie-stealing desperadoes with rib-tickling results!

GRANNY, THE BABY, AND THE BIG GRAY THING
By Peggy Parish/Illustrated by Lynn Sweat

The Indians think near-sighted Granny is going to feed their baby to a wolf. "The confusion that results makes a droll and sprightly story." —*Publishers Weekly*

TOO MANY RABBITS
By Peggy Parish/Illustrated by Leonard Kessler

How many rabbits are too many? Kind-hearted Miss Molly finds out soon enough when she takes in one stray. "Will delight primary readers."
—*School Library Journal*

THE GOLLYWHOPPER EGG
Written and illustrated by Anne Rockwell

Country peddler Timothy Todd sells a coconut as a gollywhopper egg and Farmer Foote tries to hatch it. "Fun and good humor...."
—*School Library Journal* (starred review)

A BEAR, A BOBCAT AND THREE GHOSTS
Written and illustrated by Anne Rockwell

Timothy Todd joins a moonlit Halloween chase, and "beginning readers get a comic and mysterious *Ready-to-Read.*" —*Publishers Weekly*

TIMOTHY TODD'S GOOD THINGS ARE GONE
Written and illustrated by Anne Rockwell

The peddler's pack disappears, and he sets out to find the thief. Surprises in store will delight beginning readers.